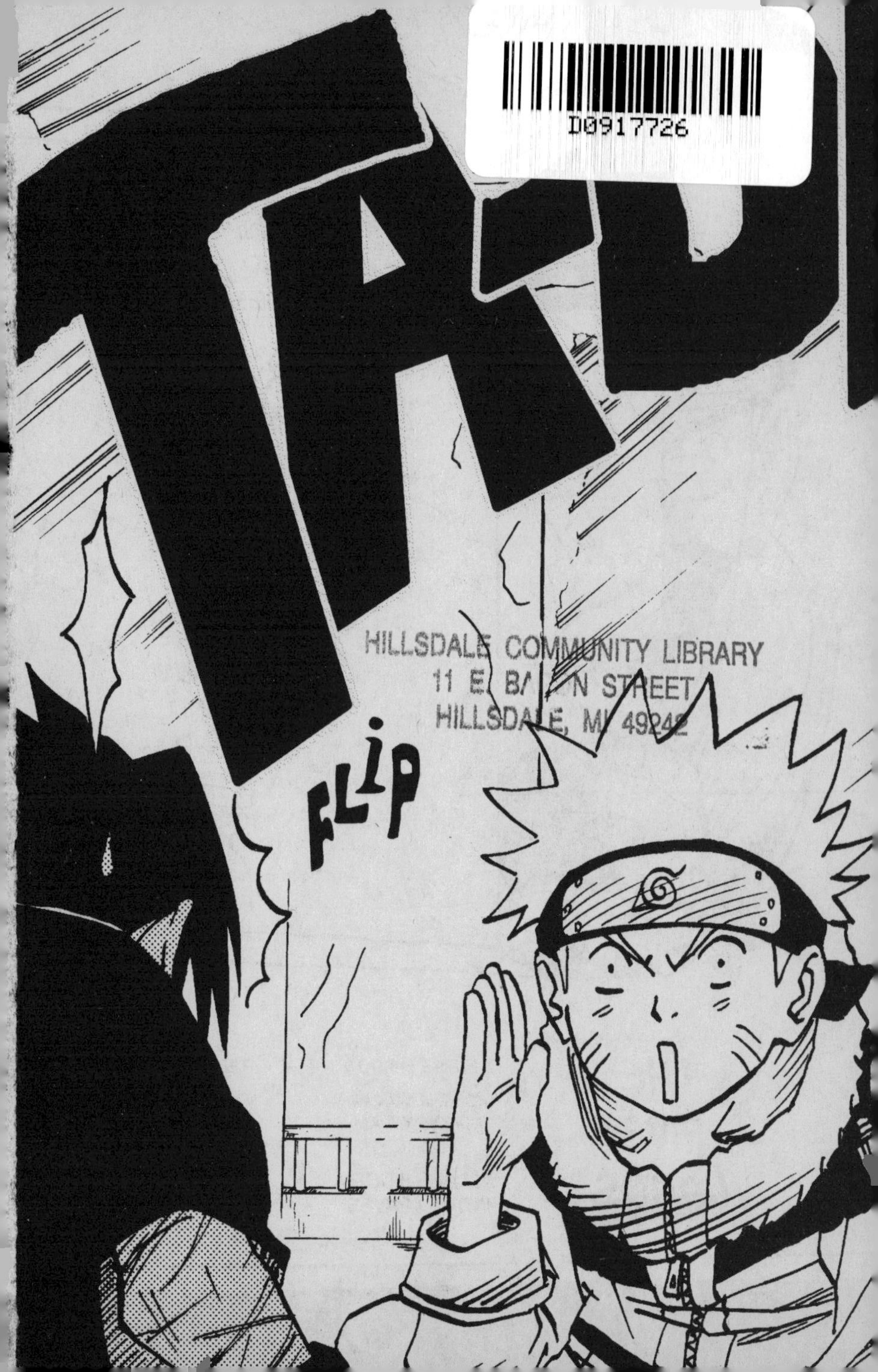
FLIP

IWA NO KUNI:
THE LAND
OF STONES

SUNA NO KUNI:
THE LAND
OF SAND

THE
FIVE
LANDS

THE FIRE SHADOW

KONOHA NO KUNI
KONOHARGURE
NO SATO:

**VILLAGE HIDDEN
IN THE LEAVES**

THE WATER SHADOW

KIRO NO KUNI
KIRIGAKURE
NO SATO:

**VILLAGE HIDDEN
IN THE MIST**

KUMO NO KUNI:
THE LAND OF
THE CLOUDS

KIRO NO KUNI:
THE LAND OF
MIST AND FOG

KONOHA NO KUNI:
THE LAND OF
TREE AND LEAF

THE LIGHTNING SHADOW

KUMO NO KUNI
KUMOGAKURE
NO SATO:

**VILLAGE HIDDEN
IN THE CLOUDS**

THE WIND SHADOW

SUNA NO KUNI
SUNAGAKURE
NO SATO:

**VILLAGE HIDDEN
IN THE SAND**

THE EARTH SHADOW

IWA NO KUNI
IWAGAKURE
NO SATO:

**VILLAGE HIDDEN
IN THE SHADOW**

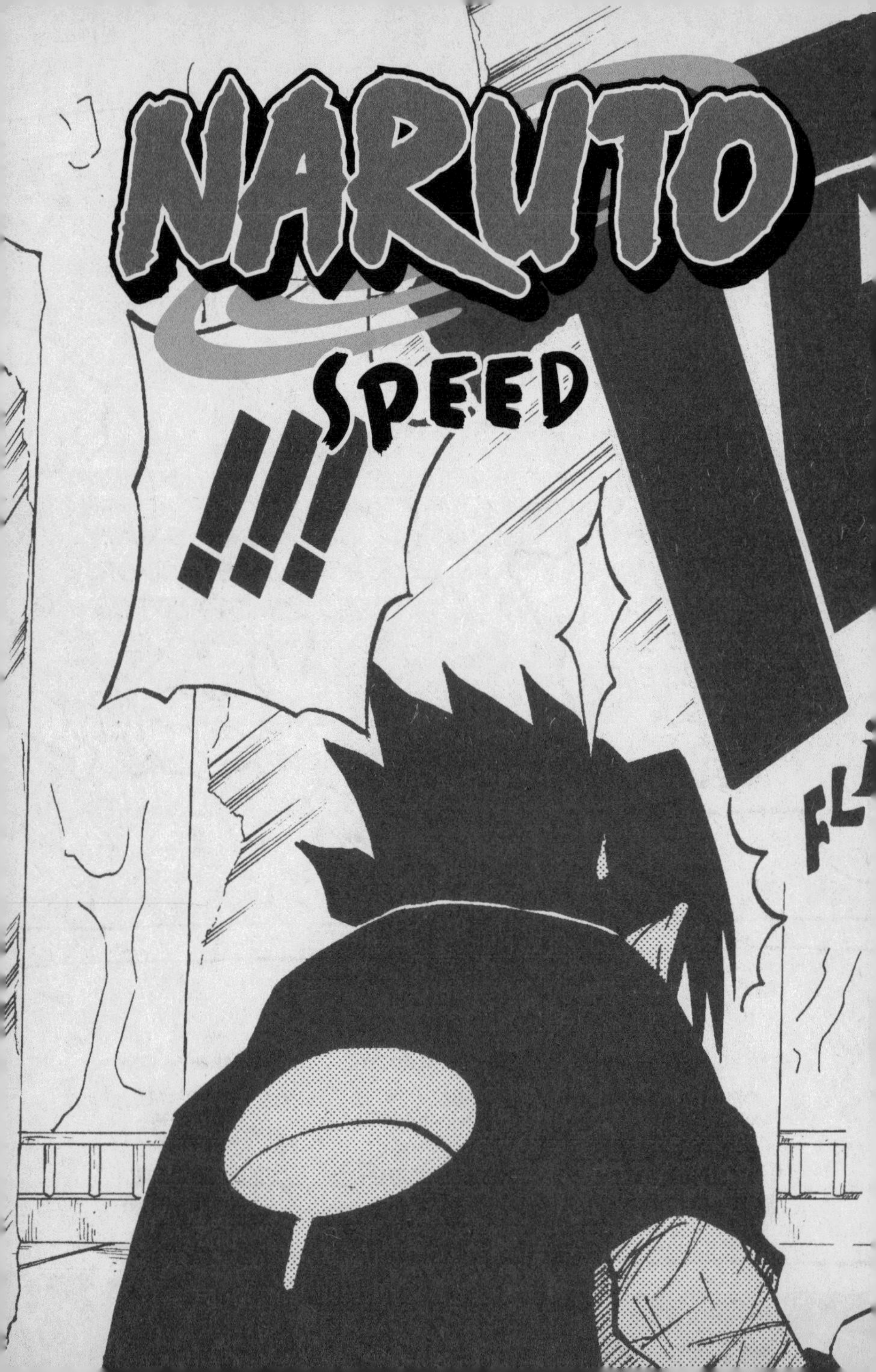
NARUTO
SPEED
!!!
FLI

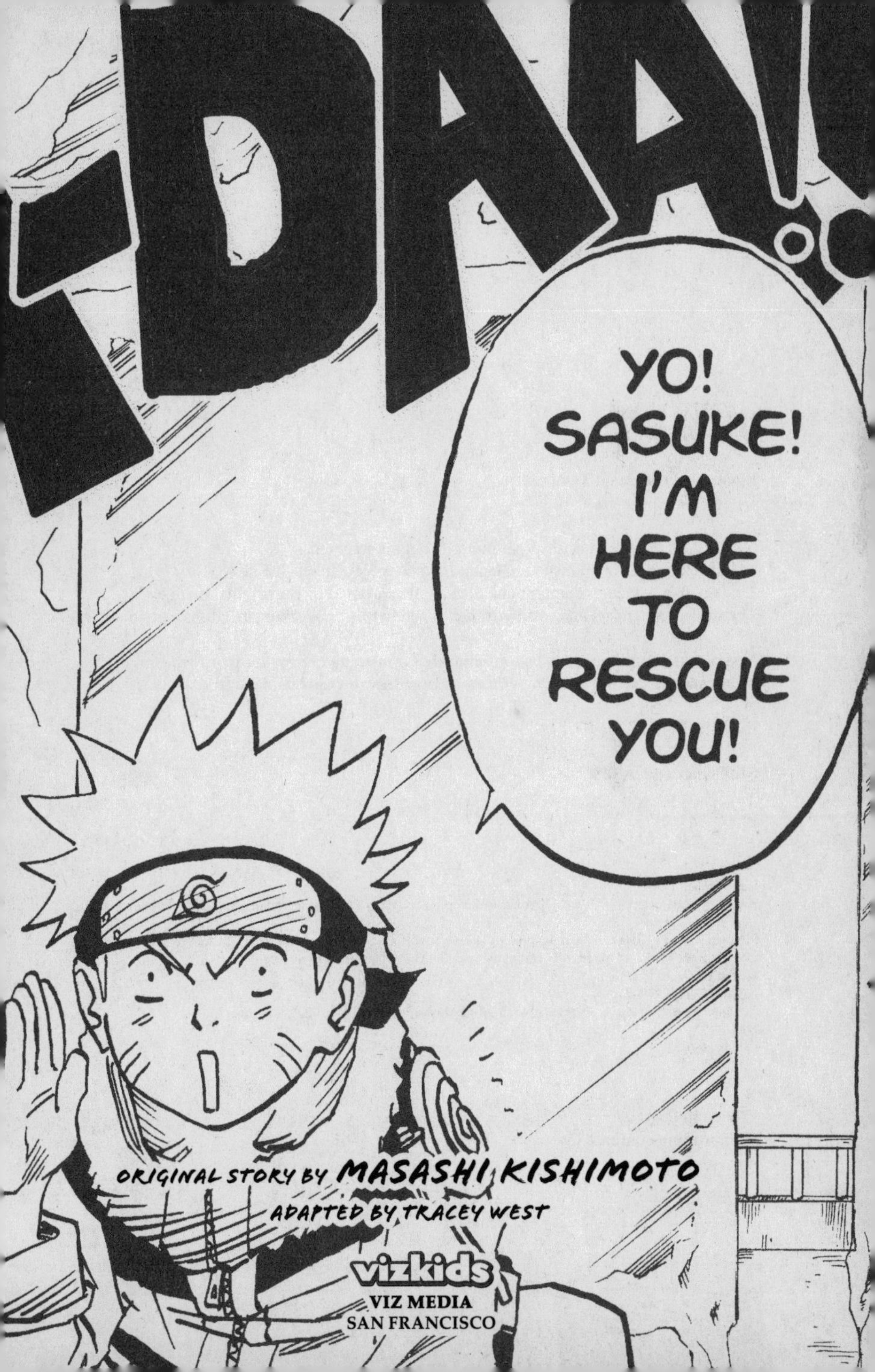
DA!
YO! SASUKE! I'M HERE TO RESCUE YOU!

ORIGINAL STORY BY MASASHI KISHIMOTO

ADAPTED BY TRACEY WEST

vizkids
VIZ MEDIA
SAN FRANCISCO

NARUTO SPEED
CHAPTER BOOK 6

Illustrations: Masashi Kishimoto
Design: Courtney Utt

Published by VIZ Media, LLC
P.O. Box 77010
San Francisco, CA 94107

www.viz.com

West, Tracey, 1965-
Speed / original story by Masashi Kishimoto ; adapted by Tracey West ; [illustrations, Masashi Kishimoto].
    p. cm. -- (Naruto)
Summary: Young ninja Naruto must protect Tazuna the bridge-builder from the evil Zabuza,
Demon of the Mist, and his partner Haku, the speediest ninja Naruto has ever faced.
ISBN-13: 978-1-4215-2316-3
ISBN-10: 1-4215-2316-7
[1. Ninja--Fiction. 2. Japan--Fiction.] I. Kishimoto, Masashi, 1974- II. Title. PZ7.W51937Sp 2009
[Fic]--dc22
    2008030322

Printed in the U.S.A.
First printing, March 2009

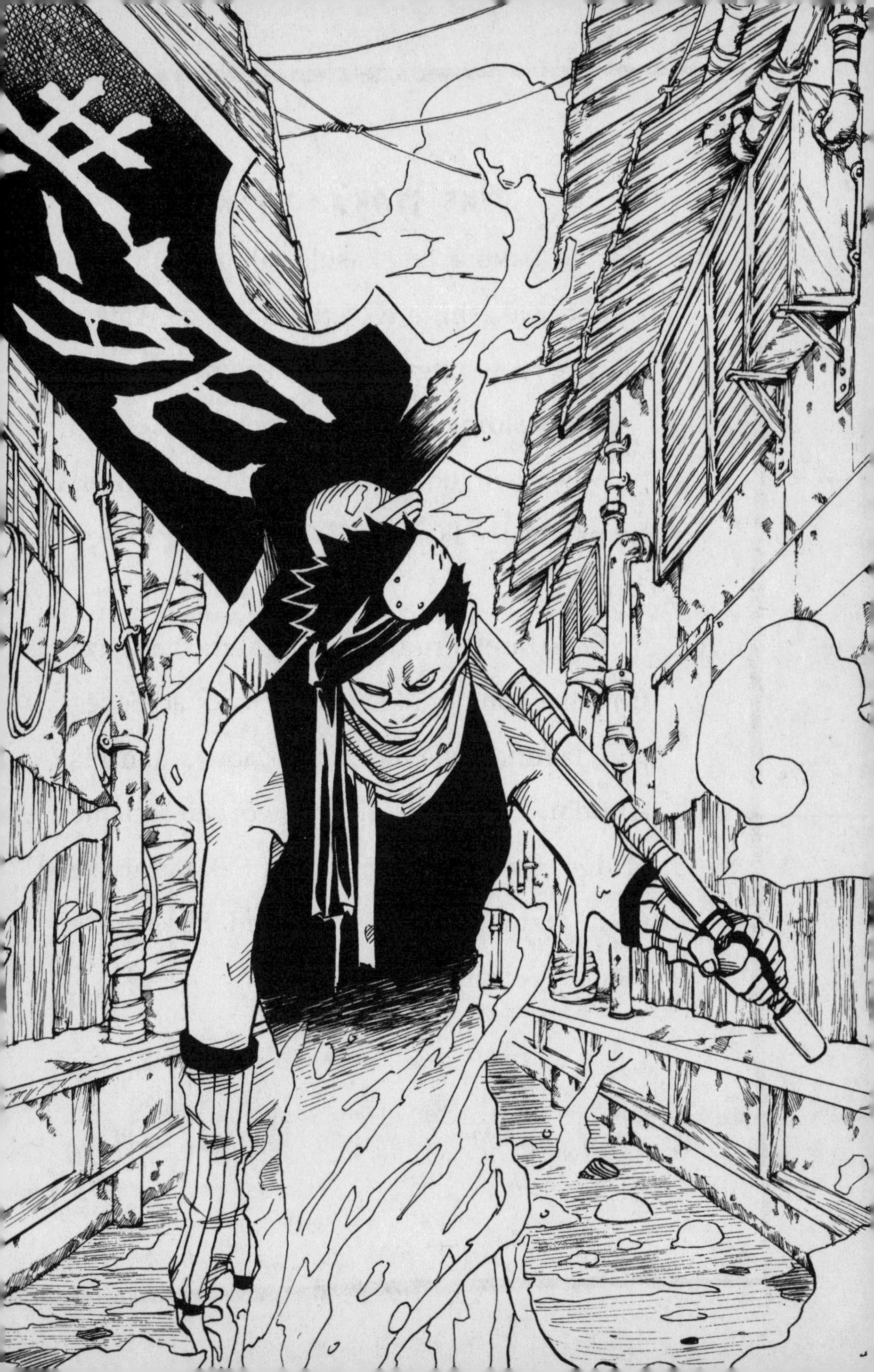

THE STORY SO FAR

Naruto, Sakura, and Sasuke, along with their leader, Kakashi, are in the Land of Waves. They're protecting an old man named Tazuna, who is building a bridge to connect the Land of Waves with other lands. A rich and powerful man named Gato will do anything to stop him.

Gato hires a ruthless ninja named Zabuza from the Land of Mist to attack Squad Seven and Tazuna. One morning, Zabuza and his student, Haku, attack the workers on the bridge. Kakashi, Sasuke, and Sakura arrive with Tazuna, and Zabuza and Haku take them by surprise.

Naruto
ナルト

Naruto is training to be a ninja. He's a bit of a clown. But deep down, he's serious about becoming the world's greatest shinobi!

Sakura
春野サクラ

Naruto and Sasuke's classmate. She has a crush on Sasuke, who ignores her. In return, she picks on Naruto, who has a crush on *her*.

Sasuke
うちはサスケ

The top student in Naruto's class and a member of the prestigious Uchiha clan.

THE MORNING sun cast a pale glow across the gray sky above the bridge.

Kakashi, the sensei and leader of Squad Seven, stood on the bridge. He was flanked by two of his students, Sakura and Sasuke, and Tazuna, a bearded old bridge builder.

The four of them faced two ninja who stood further down. Zabuza, from the Land of Mist, wore black pants and a black tank top. A white cloth mask covered his mouth and nose. Black hair spiked up above his

Land of Mist headband. His giant sword was strapped across his back.

"I see you've got your little brats with you, Kakashi," Zabuza taunted.

Next to Zabuza stood Haku, who was shorter and not as muscular as Zabuza. He wore a kimono. Over his face was the mask of the ninja hunter, a white mask with a swirl design on it.

Kakashi and the others had seen Haku before. When they first met, Haku had claimed to be a ninja hunter sent to stop Zabuza. But Kakashi didn't trust that story.

"Looks like I was right," Kakashi said. He wore a black mask over the lower half of his face. His Leaf Village headband covered his left eye.

"Oh!" gasped Sakura, her pale eyes wide.

Kakashi nodded. "Our mysterious masked friend is playing on Zabuza's team."

"He's got some nerve, showing up here like this!" Tazuna said in his gruff voice.

Sasuke's dark eyes clouded. The young ninja stepped forward. When they arrived at the bridge, Zabuza had attacked with his water clones. Sasuke had easily seen through the illusion. He got rid of them quickly, all by himself.

"That was quite a show you put on before," Sasuke said, his voice steady. "But we're onto you now—and I hate show-offs."

Sakura gazed at him. "Sasuke's so cool!" she said under her breath.

Kakashi shook his head. *Sakura, don't you*

realize Sasuke is a show-off too?

Haku studied Sasuke. "Impressive, isn't he?" he told Zabuza. "Even if your water clones were only one-tenth as strong as usual, it was amazing he was able to do so well."

"But we're still on the attack," Zabuza reminded Haku. "GO!"

"Yes, sir!" Haku replied.

Haku began to move down the bridge, twirling in circles. His feet moved so quickly that the ninja looked like a small tornado bearing down on them.

Sasuke held steady. What kind of attack was this? He gripped his kunai, waiting for the exact right moment to move.

If he took his eyes off of Haku for even a second, the battle would be over.

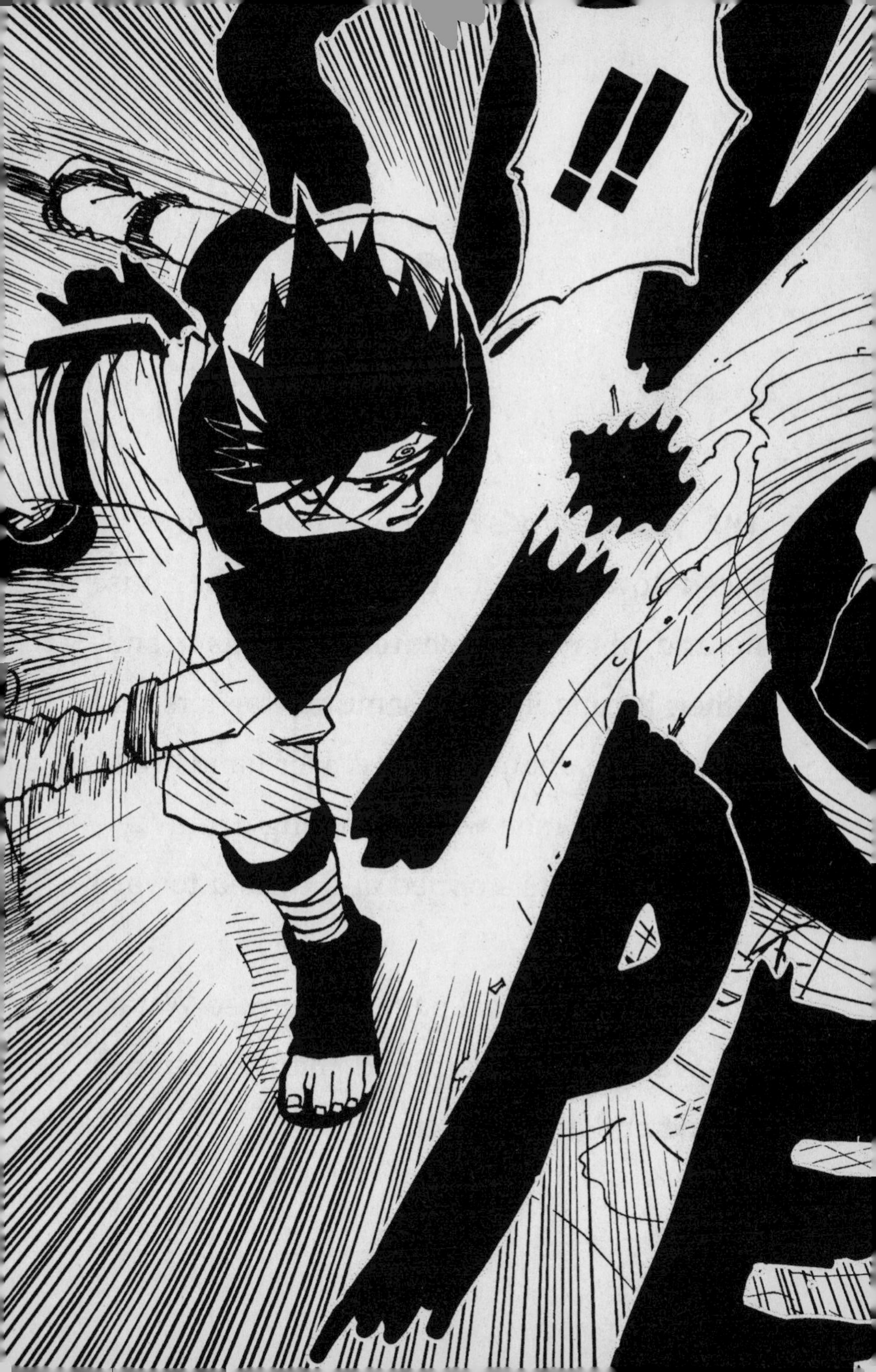
!!

THE YOUNG boy's heart was pounding as he raced down the dock that led from the house he and his mother shared with his grand-father, Tazuna. Two big samurai warriors held his mom, Tsunami, captive. Her hands were tied, and the men were marching her away.

The warriors stopped and turned toward Inari.

"This kid is a real pain," remarked Waraji. He was a huge, tattooed man wearing a sarong and an eyepatch.

"Yeah," agreed Zouri. He wore a knit cap over his dark gray hair and was dressed in a gray military-style jacket. He drew his sword and glared at Inari. "Let's get him."

"Inari, no!" Tsunami yelled. Waraji roughly pushed her down.

The boy didn't stop. He charged at the two samurai. Their swords gleamed in the sunlight as they slashed at Inari…

…and cut right through a log instead!

YOU GET AWAY FROM MY MAMA--!!

YES, I CAN...!!

Y.

Puzzled, the samurai watched as the sliced-up log clattered onto the dock.

"The Art of Substitution?" Zouri said in disbelief. How did a small boy know such a difficult move?

"Sorry I'm late!"

The hired warriors slowly turned to look behind them. They saw a young ninja with spiky yellow hair wearing an orange jumpsuit. The boy had Inari in his arms, and he

ing Tsunami, who lay motionless
ck.

"Heroes always come in the nick of time,"
Naruto told Inari, grinning.

"N-Naruto?" Inari asked, confused.

The samurai were confused too. "Isn't that
one of Tazuna's low budget bodyguards?"

Naruto ignored them. "You did great,
Inari," he told the boy. "While you distracted
them, I was able to grab your mom. Then I
used a replacement jutsu to fool those guys
into thinking that log was you."

The samurai were angry now. They raced
down the dock after Naruto.

"Naruto, will you be okay?" Inari asked.

"No sweat," Naruto replied. He reached
into a pouch strapped to his leg and pulled

out two throwing stars. Then he threw them at the warriors as they bore down.

SHIING! SHIING! The samurai expertly blocked the shuriken with their sword handles.

"Hah! Did you really expect these to take us down?" Waraji scoffed.

Naruto just smiled. "Suckers!"

Two clones of Naruto appeared behind the samurai. The clones were solid copies of Naruto—and they had the same skills he had.

POW! Each Naruto delivered a powerful kick to the heads of the two samurai. Waraji and Zouri fell over, knocked out cold.

Inari stared wide-eyed at the fallen men. They were both much bigger and taller than

Naruto. But Naruto had beaten them both!

"Naruto, how'd you know the samurai were here?" Inari asked.

"There was a wild pig back in the forest, cut to ribbons with a sword," Naruto explained. "And trees with fresh deep slashes in their bark, going in the direction of your house. It wasn't too hard to figure out. But forget that."

Naruto faced Inari. "I owe you an apology."

"Why?" Inari asked.

Naruto blushed a little, which made the strange whisker-like marks on his cheeks stand out. "Well, um, I'm sorry I called you a baby," he said. Naruto was remembering an argument he and Inari had the night before.

Inari thought Squad Seven wasn't strong enough to face Zabuza, and Naruto had lashed out at the boy.

"It's not true, okay?" Naruto said. He patted Inari on the head. "You're a big, strong boy!"

A strange feeling came over Inari. His eyes filled with tears. He tried to hold them back, but they rolled down his cheeks.

"Oh no!" Inari wailed. "I promised myself I wouldn't cry. Now you'll make fun of me again!"

"No way!" Naruto promised. He remembered the last time he had cried. It wasn't because he was sad.

The adults in Naruto's village all knew a secret about him—the spirit of the Nine-Tailed Demon Fox was trapped inside his

body. They treated Naruto like an outcast—
except for his teacher, Master Iruka. He made
Naruto feel accepted for the very first time,
and when that happened, Naruto had cried
tears of happiness.

Naruto folded his hands behind his head
and smiled at Inari. "Nothing wrong with
CRYING when you're *HAPPY*!" he said.

Inari was stunned for a moment. For the
first time in a long time, somebody finally
understood him. He started to cry again.

Inari watched Naruto quickly tie up the
two samurai. "So if they attacked us here, it
means the bridge is probably a target too,"
he said. He glanced back at Inari. "You can
handle things here, right?"

"Yeah," Inari replied. He dried his tears on

his sleeve.

Naruto and Inari pounded fists. "Man, this hero thing is a lot of work!" Naruto said.

"**YOU BET!**" Inari agreed.

SASUKE TENSED as Haku whirled toward him like a tornado. Suddenly Haku was upon him! Haku struck with a kunai. Sasuke blocked the blow with his own kunai.

CHING! The clash of metal on metal echoed across the bridge.

He can keep up with Haku's speed, Zabuza realized.

Kakashi looked thoughtful. He had to keep his eyes on Zabuza. The ninja could strike at any time.

"Sakura, we have to cover Mr. Tazuna," Kakashi said. "Take that side and stay close! Let Sasuke handle Haku."

"Yes, sir!" Sakura replied.

Haku tried to strike Sasuke again. Again Sasuke blocked the blow. Over and over Haku tried, but Sasuke met every attack.

"I don't want to have to hurt you. But I guess you won't just give up, will you?" Haku asked.

"Don't be stupid," Sasuke spat back.

"Just as I thought," Haku said calmly. "However, you won't be able to match my speed for long. I've laid the groundwork for two attacks."

"Two attacks?" Sasuke asked. He quickly took in the scene. He and Haku were locked in a standstill. Sasuke held a kunai in his right hand, blocking a blow from Haku's right hand. It looked like a draw to Sasuke.

"First, there's the water splashed all around us," Haku explained. Sasuke glanced down at the ground. It was true. Small puddles of water covered the bridge.

"Secondly, I've trapped one of your hands with this move, which leaves you with only one hand free to defend yourself from an attack," Haku went on.

Haku raised his left hand in front of his face. He began to make hand signs with his fingers.

What? Sasuke was shocked. *The most powerful ninja moves were made by making signals with* two *hands.*

Even Kakashi was shocked. *He's making signs with just one hand? I've never seen anything like it!*

Haku's left hand moved so quickly that the signs were just a blur. He ended by holding up two fingers in front of his face.

"Secret Art of Water! **The Thousand Stinging Needles of Death!**" Haku cried.

Haku began to stomp in the puddles. The water splashed up, transforming into sharp, shimmering blue needles. The water needles

THE THOUSAND STINGING NEEDLES OF DEATH!

SECRET ART OF WATER!

formed a circle around Sasuke and Haku.

"Sasuke!" Sakura screamed. She knew what was coming. Another stamp of Haku's foot would send the needles flying into Sasuke.

Sasuke closed his eyes. He remembered training in the woods with Kakashi, learning how to control the energy inside his body called chakra. *Come on! Gotta remember the training.*

Haku stomped his foot, sending the needles flying.

I must summon all of the chakra energy I can, Sasuke thought. *AND FOCUS IT IN MY FEET!*

WHOOSH! Sasuke rocketed into the air, above the needles. There was a splash as the needles turned back into harmless water droplets and hit the bridge.

Sasuke was gone.

Where did he go? Haku wondered.

He heard a sound and looked up.

SASUKE!!

A rain of shuriken fell from the sky. *Thuk thuk thuk!* Haku dodged the throwing stars, avoiding them with a back flip. When he landed, he heard a voice behind him.

"You're not that fast," said Sasuke. "Now you're the one who has to worry about defending yourself from *my* attacks."

Sasuke picked up Haku and flipped him, slamming him to the ground.

He's fast! Haku realized in surprise.

POW! Sasuke kicked Haku. The ninja skidded across the bridge and landed at Zabuza's feet.

Zabuza couldn't believe what he was seeing. *Haku is actually losing a battle of speed?*

"You're fast, but I'm faster," Sasuke said.

"You had that coming for insulting my

team," Kakashi said. "He may not look like much, but Sasuke here is the top-rated rookie in the Leaf Village. And Sakura here is our sharpest mind."

Sakura blushed modestly. But her Inner Sakura was a lot more confident.

That's right! You said it!

"And last but not least, let's not forget our comedy ninja, that unpredictable show-off, Naruto," Kakashi finished.

Zabuza chuckled. "Haku, do you understand if this goes on, he could get you instead?"

Haku rose to his feet. "Yes, I do," he replied, his voice cold. "What a pity."

Sasuke noticed something else cold too— the air around him. Haku lowered his hand

and made another hand sign. He pressed his palms together and crossed his index fingers.

A crackling sound filled the air as the puddles rose again.

"SECRET ART OF WATER! **MAGIC CRYSTAL** ICE MIRROR!" Haku cried.

The water formed thin walls of ice that trapped Sasuke inside. Cold air chilled his arms. An eerie silence surrounded him. He watched as Haku slowly stepped into one of the walls and became one with the ice.

An image of Haku appeared on every frozen panel. To Sasuke it looked like he was in a house of mirrors, but instead of seeing his own reflection, he saw Haku.

Kakashi sprang toward the ice walls, but

Zabuza jumped in front of him, blocking his way.

"Don't forget, I'm your enemy," Zabuza said. "He's as good as dead once Haku uses that jutsu."

Inside, Sasuke gazed around him, trying to figure out what to do. Then Haku's voice echoed through the frozen jail.

"Let me show you some *SPEED!*"

The attack seemed to come from everywhere at once. Haku slashed at him with a long, sharp needle. Sasuke tried to block the blows, but he couldn't stop them all. He cried out in panic.

Sakura's eyes burned with anger. "Mr. Tazuna, I'm sorry, but I'm going to have to leave you for a little bit."

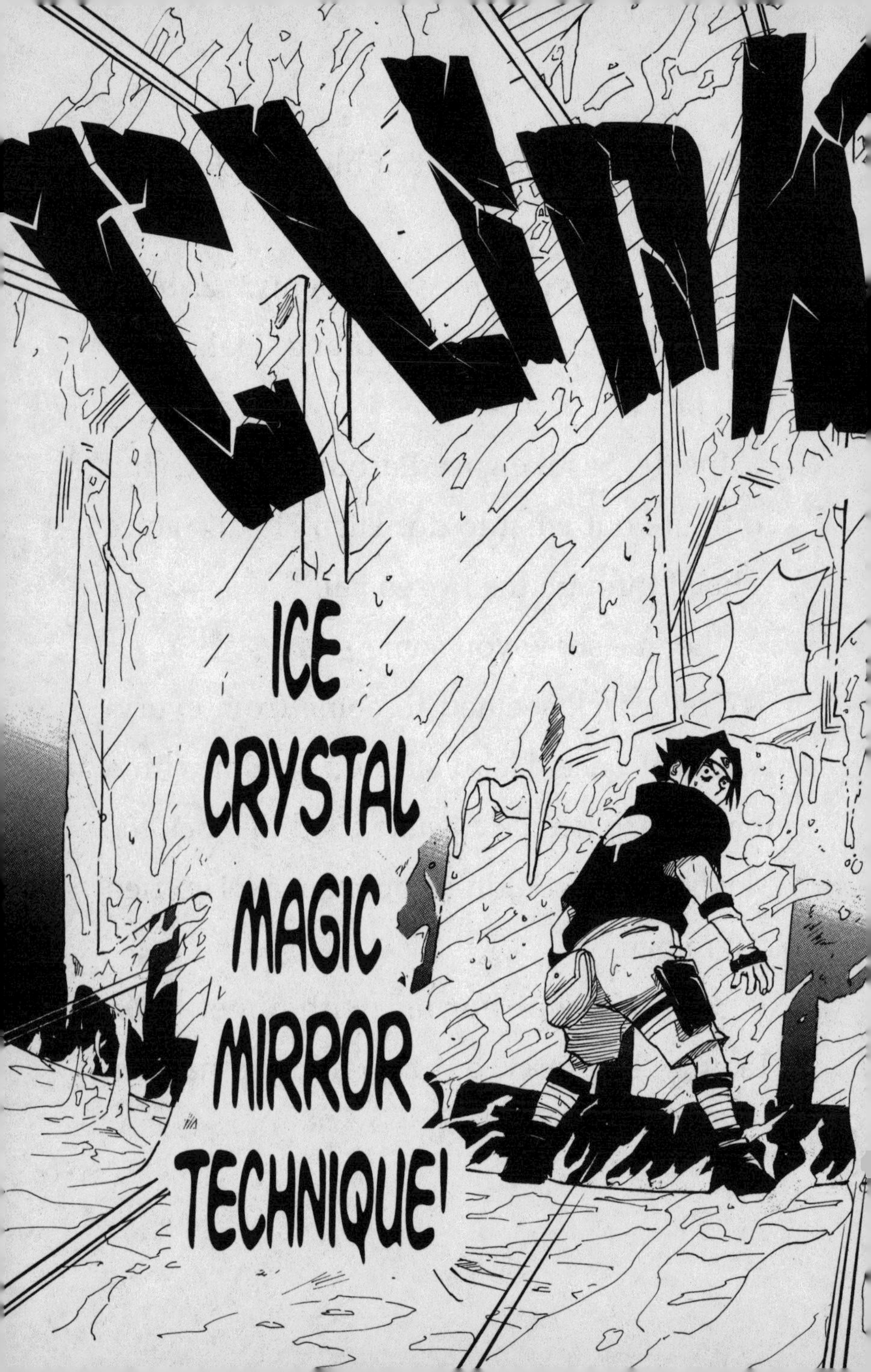
ICE CRYSTAL MAGIC MIRROR TECHNIQUE!

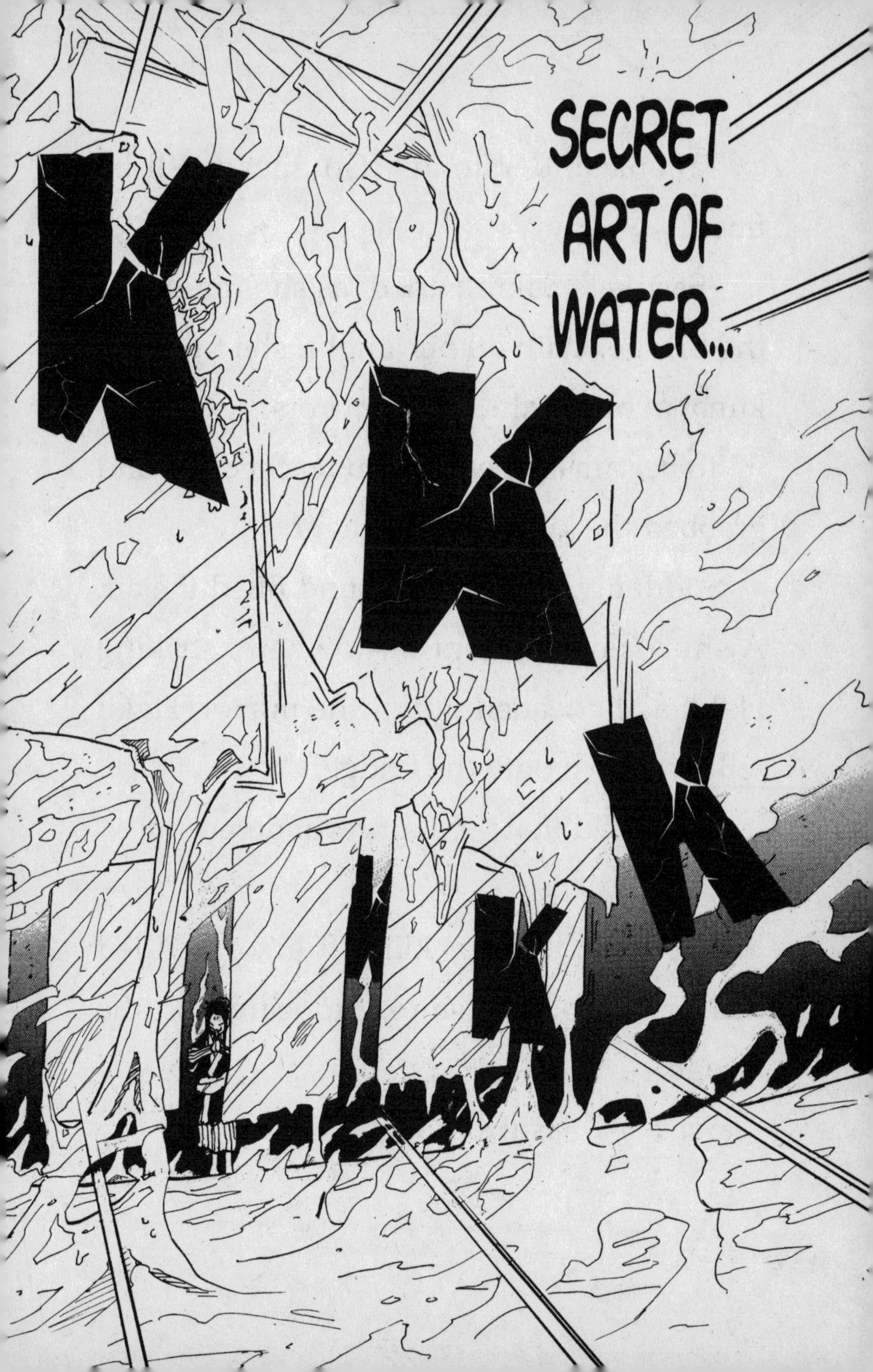
SECRET ART OF WATER...

Tazuna understood. "Go ahead. I'll be fine."

"Sasuke!" Sakura cried, as she ran down the bridge. With all her might, she hurled a kunai at one of the Haku mirrors.

To her amazement, Haku reached out and grabbed the kunai in mid-flight.

Suddenly, a whirring sound filled the air. A shuriken came out of nowhere, striking Haku as he leaned out of the mirror. Haku fell facedown onto the bridge.

"Who did that?" Sakura wondered.

POOF!

The sound of crackling fireworks filled the air. A cloud of smoke appeared on the bridge.

Show-off! Sasuke thought.

Plumes of smoke billowed from the bridge now. Naruto jumped out of the smoke, making hand signs above his head and in front of his face.

"NARUTO UZUMAKI, AT YOUR SERVICE!"

4

"I'M HERE to save the day!" Naruto cried, pointing at Haku. "You know how the story goes. Things look bleak until the hero arrives. And then POW! Bye-bye bad guys."

Kakashi sighed. *What we needed was an ambush. Instead, he bursts in here, all fired up. He might as well have painted a target on himself!*

Sakura was impressed. "Naruto!" she cheered.

Big talker! Sasuke thought.

Haku eyed Naruto curiously. The day

before, Haku had met Naruto in the woods. Haku wasn't wearing his mask, and Naruto hadn't recognized him.

Hmph! This brat again? Zabuza wondered. The last time he had battled Kakashi and his team, Naruto had caused him some trouble. His eyes narrowed as he reached for his weapons.

Kakashi sensed the move too late. Zabuza sent a storm of shuriken hurling toward Naruto.

Here it comes, Naruto thought. He held

his kunai in front of him, ready to defend himself.

But he didn't have to. Behind him, Haku threw out a number of shuriken. They flew through the air, knocking down the attacking shuriken one by one.

CHING! CHING! CHING! CHING!

Naruto watched, stunned, as the shuriken clattered harmlessly to the ground.

"Haku, what are you doing?" Zabuza yelled.

"Zabuza, sir, please let me have at this boy," Haku said, bowing his head in respect. "I want to fight him in my own way."

"So you want me to keep my hands off him?" Zabuza asked. "You may try, but you're wrong, as usual."

Sasuke was glad for the distraction. He knew he had to figure out the secret of the ice mirror trick if he wanted to beat Haku—unless Naruto could free him from outside first.

"Ta-daaaaa!"

Sasuke looked up. Naruto was right in front of him!

"Yo, Sasuke! I'm here to rescue you!" Naruto said. He held his hand to his mouth, like he was whispering, but everyone on the bridge heard him.

"You doofus!" Sasuke yelled. "A ninja is supposed to move quietly, with stealth. Now you've gotten yourself trapped in here with me!"

Leave it to the team rebel, Kakashi thought.

Once Naruto starts "helping," things go from bad to worse. And if I go help the boys, Mr. Tazuna will be completely exposed.

I could use my Shadow Clone, but Zabuza would just counter with his Water Clones. I'd be wasting my chakra.

While Kakashi tried to figure out a strategy, Haku stepped back into the wall of ice. Sasuke saw Haku appear on a mirror in front of him.

So that's where his real body is, Sasuke guessed. He reached for his kunai.

Then he heard a voice behind him. "Over here."

Sasuke turned. But how could that be?

"What the heck is going on?" Naruto yelled.

Looks like destroying all the mirrors may be our only hope, Sasuke thought. *These mirrors are made of ice, so...*

"FIRE STYLE!" Sasuke yelled.

He quickly made a hand sign, and a circle of angry orange flames rose up around him. "Fireball Jutsu!"

But the impressive fire died out.

"It's not even making a dent!" Naruto said.

"That pitiful flame will barely touch my ice mirrors," Haku said. He drew his kunai, and before the boys could react, all of the Haku clones slashed at them. Naruto rolled on the floor, trying to avoid the sharp needles.

Where's the attack coming from? Are they all clones? he wondered. "Which one of you is real?" Naruto shouted.

"Your eyes will never see the truth," Haku replied. "I can't be caught."

"Ha!" Naruto cried. He made a hand sign in front of his face.

"Art of the Doppelganger!"

Sasuke turned to him, panicked. *"STOP!"*

NARUTO DIDN'T listen. In a flash, the entire house of mirrors was filled with clones of Naruto.

Bam! Bam! Bam!

The clones kicked the mirrors, trying to shatter them.

If I clobber every one of him, then sooner or later I'll get to the real one! Naruto thought.

From the corner of his eye, Naruto saw Haku emerge from one of the mirrors. He held a long, sharp needle in his hand. With a cry, Naruto jumped up and flew toward the mirror, his fist clenched.

WHOOSH!

Haku raced past him so quickly all Naruto saw was a blur. Haku zipped back and forth across the icy room, attacking each of the Naruto clones one by one.

POW! POW! POW! POW! POW!

"Auuuuuuugh!" Naruto screamed. He landed on the slick floor and skidded to a stop. Haku had destroyed every one of his clones!

"The technique I'm using is part of the Art of Teleportation, and the only tool I need to perform it is the mirrors that hold my image," Haku explained. "I move so quickly, the pair of you might as well be standing still."

"So that's it!" Kakashi said. "I never imagined that anyone could master such a technique at so young an age."

Zabuza gave a low chuckle.

"Such a technique?" Sakura asked.

"It's a kekkei genkai—a skill that can be passed from one generation to the next," Kakashi replied. "It is passed through the bloodlines of some of the most expert ninja. Some of the greatest moves can only be inherited this way. There's no other way to learn them."

Sakura's eyes widened. "You mean..."

"Exactly. It's the same kind of skill as my

Sharingan Mirror Eye," Kakashi said. The sensei spoke of the power in his left eye, the eye he kept covered by his headband. The eye gave Kakashi the power to instantly master an opponent's attack and use it against him.

"But even my Sharingan can't copy this boy's move," Kakashi said.

Inside the icy prison, Naruto glared at Haku.

"I've had enough," he said. "It can't end like this. I've got a dream to fulfill!"

Naruto longed to become the world's greatest ninja. Then the people of the Leaf Village would have to look up to him!

"I find it hard to accept the way of the ninja," Haku replied. "I would rather not have to hurt you both. However, if you are going to attack me, I shall ignore my heart and defend myself with every skill I have."

Haku's soft voice grew stronger and louder as he spoke. "This bridge is where our destinies meet," he went on. "I have my own dreams as you have yours. My dream is to protect the one I care about most. And that's Zabuza. To do that, I will become a true ninja. I will destroy you both!"

Haku's words lit a fire in Sasuke's and Naruto's eyes. If Haku wanted a fight, they were ready.

"Sasuke! Naruto! Don't you dare lose to him!" Sakura yelled.

"Stop encouraging them, Sakura!" Kakashi warned. "Even if we knew a way to counter his move, your teammates still couldn't beat that boy."

"What do you mean?" Sakura asked.

Zabuza laughed.

"Those two don't have the heart to destroy another person," Kakashi told her. "They haven't yet learned to turn their hearts to ice."

"No true ninja could ever be born in your village, a place of peace," Zabuza scoffed. "None of you have lived with death or grown up struggling to survive."

Sakura clenched her fists. If Kakashi was right, then winning this battle was impossible!

"Master Kakashi, what can we do?" she cried.

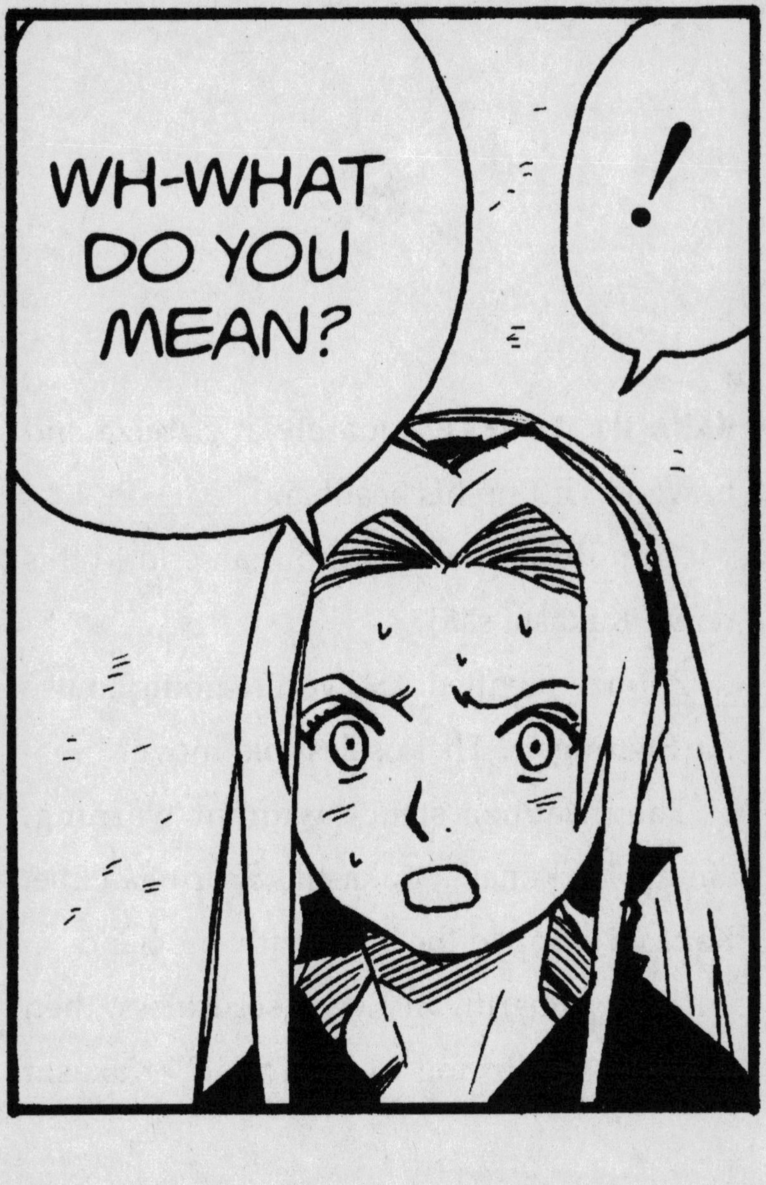
!
WH-WHAT DO YOU MEAN?

6

KAKASHI LOOKED squarely at Zabuza and moved to lift up his headband.

"You'll forgive me if I put an end to this now," Kakashi said.

Zabuza laughed. "So you're going to use the Sharingan? That useless old move?"

Then Zabuza struck without warning, aiming his kunai at Kakashi's Sharingan Eye. Kakashi stopped the blow with one hand.

"If my Sharingan Eye is so useless, then why are you trying to destroy it?" Kakashi asked. "Admit it, Zabuza. You're afraid."

"A move like that is a ninja's secret weapon," Zabuza replied. "You shouldn't use it on every enemy you face."

"You should feel lucky. No one else has lived to see the Sharingan Eye twice," Kakashi said.

Zabuza just laughed again. "Defeat me if you can. You still won't be able to beat Haku!"

Is it true? Is that masked boy so powerful that even Master Kakashi can't win? Sakura wondered.

"I have trained Haku to be a ninja ever since he was a small boy," Zabuza went on. "His skills are even better than mine. And his kekkei genkai—the move he inherited—makes

...IF I PUT AN END TO THIS...!

YOU'LL FORGIV ME...

him extremely powerful."

Zabuza slashed at Kakashi with the kunai once again. "In Haku, I have a skilled weapon that I bring with me everywhere. All you have are those little scraps of trash who follow you around!"

Kakashi blocked the blow. "Is there

anything more boring than listening to someone else brag?" he asked.

He lifted up his headband, revealing his
Sharingan Eye. Strange black symbols swirled
inside the eye's blood red iris.

ONNNNNNNNNNNNG! The power of
the move echoed across the bridge.

"It's showtime!" Kakashi cried.

"I remember something you said at our
last encounter," Zabuza said. "Frankly, I've
been dying to steal it."

Sakura, Tazuna, and Kakashi watched
Zabuza, curious. What was he talking
about?

Zabuza grinned behind his mask. "The
same spell won't work on me twice!"

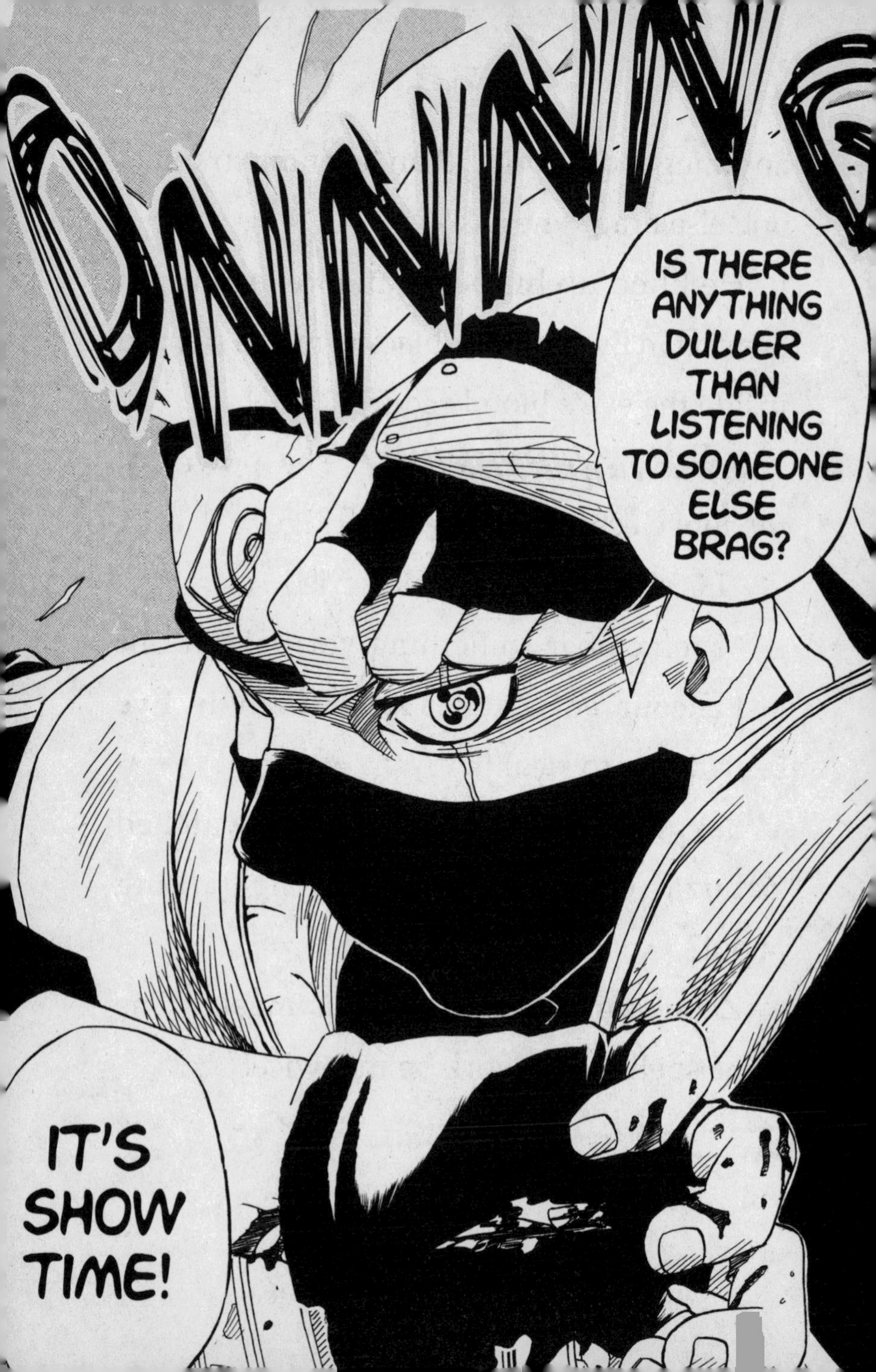
DNNNNG
IS THERE ANYTHING DULLER THAN LISTENING TO SOMEONE ELSE BRAG?
IT'S SHOW TIME!

"AFTER SEEING your Sharingan Eye in action, I think I know how it works," Zabuza went on. "Haku was hidden while we fought and saw the battle from beginning to end."

Zabuza reached for his giant sword. The blade was almost as long as Zabuza was tall.

"And now—the Art of Hiding in the Mist!" Zabuza cried out.

Kakashi tensed as a thick, gray mist covered the bridge. Zabuza had used this move the last time they battled. He could move through the mist, hidden, and then attack without warning.

"Sakura! I'm counting on you to protect Mr. Tazuna!" Kakashi called out.

He's right, Sakura realized. *I've got to have faith in Sasuke and concentrate on what I have to do!*

"Where the heck is that fog coming from?" the bridge builder complained. "You can't see your hand in front of your face!"

Sakura moved closer to him and tightly gripped her kunai. "The air is crackling with his energy, Mr. Tazuna. Stay by my side!" she ordered.

The old man nodded. "All right, Sakura!"

Kakashi waited, watching and listening

for Zabuza to make a move.

This fog is too thick for the Art of Hiding in the Mist technique, Kakashi thought. *Even Zabuza won't be able to see anything!*

Then Kakashi heard a noise. Something was flying toward him. He quickly raised his kunai in defense.

CHING! CHING! CHING! CHING! CHING!

With lightning speed, he used his kunai to repel each shuriken. Then he heard Zabuza's voice behind him.

"Nice job. Just what I'd expect from Kakashi of the Sharingan Eye."

Kakashi turned to face his enemy. Zabuza's eyes were closed.

"Next time you see me, it will be the end," Zabuza said. "Your Sharingan is useless

against me now."

Zabuza disappeared into the thick mist once more.

"What?" Kakashi wondered.

Zabuza's laugh cut through the fog. "You pretend that your eye allows you to see all. But you can't read my mind, and you can't read the future either. I've figured out your trick. You use your eye to quickly copy my movements. Then, when I'm out in the open, you lay your trap. You hypnotize me to trick me into signaling what technique I'll use and how I'll be doing it. Then all you have to do is mimic it!"

Kakashi stayed still, waiting for Zabuza to stop talking and make his move. Suddenly he felt the ninja race past him, knocking him over.

"Ha!" Zabuza laughed. "If I keep my eyes closed, you can't hypnotize me."

"But with your eyes closed, you can't see," Kakashi pointed out.

"Ah, you forget," Zabuza replied. "I can hunt you by sound alone!"

Oh no! Kakashi thought. *I've been so worried about Naruto and Sasuke. I forgot how long* it's been since I've had to fight under these conditions. I've got to calm down and stay smart. Who will he target next?

Shoom!

Kakashi turned. "No!"

Zabuza appeared out of the mist, right behind Tazuna! He raised his sword to strike. Kakashi raced to put himself between the bridge builder and the ninja.

Zabuza brought down his sword. "Too late!"

SASUKE AND Naruto heard Sakura scream.

What's happening out there? Sasuke wondered. *What is Kakashi doing? I've got to do something!*

Haku studied the boys. Both of them were tired and hurt from Haku's attacks. Sasuke made him curious.

He is able to dodge many of my moves, Haku realized. *And while he's dividing his own focus between fighting me and watching out for his friend, he's gaining speed. He's even starting to catch up to my moves. That kid can see something!* Sasuke stood up, holding back a groan. He glared at Haku's reflection in the mirrors.

"You move well," Haku told him. "But my next assault will take you down."

Sasuke steeled his nerves as he got ready for the next attack.

Here he comes, Sasuke told himself. *Focus! Look through the illusion.*

Fwooooosh! Haku jumped out of a mirror and aimed a slew of needles at Sasuke. Sasuke jumped out of the way, avoiding most of the sharp weapons. He fell to the ground in a heap.

Impossible! Haku thought. *He wasn't fooled or even confused!*

Sasuke raised his head and growled

at Haku. The masked ninja gasped. Both
of Sasuke's eyes were red. Black symbols
swirled inside them.

It can't be! Haku thought. *His eyes…they're
Sharingan!*

"I see you too have a power from a kekkei
genkai bloodline," Haku said.

Sasuke felt his energy surge as his

awakened power filled him. *It was only for a moment, but I was actually able to see!*

"I can't let this fight go on," Haku said. "My own art forces me to use a great deal of chakra, so I can't use it for much longer. And I know that the longer our duel drags on, the more you will be able to see my movements."

Haku bowed his head. He held his left hand in front of his chest and raised his right hand next to his head. Each hand gripped four sharp needles.

"TIME TO BRING THIS TO AN END!" Haku cried. He flew out of the mirror, aimed right at Naruto.

Sasuke leaped forward. *No! I have to get there first!*

"Master Kakashi!" Sakura screamed.

Kakashi blocked Zabuza's sword. The giant blade slashed through his vest, wounding him.

"You were slow on your guard, Kakashi!" Zabuza said. "Your desire to save those brats clouded your vision."

The ninja lifted his sword. "Even with your Sharingan Eye and all its powers, you can't read my movements! Haku will take care of those two brats of yours, and then I'll take care of you. I want to enjoy this, Kakashi. Paying back what you did to me will make me so happy!"

"Sasuke won't be so easy to defeat!" Sakura shouted angrily. "Neither will Naruto!"

Oh yeah! That's right! her Inner Sakura

screamed.

"You're right," Kakashi agreed, to everyone's surprise. "I have faith in them and their strengths. Naruto's unpredictable nature can be useful. And Sasuke is one of the most worthy members of the best ninja family in the Leaf Village!"

Zabuza was shocked. "You don't mean..."

"That's right," Kakashi said. "His full name is Sasuke Uchiha. He's a ninja genius who carries in his genes the kekkei genkai of the Uchiha clan!"

"So he's the last of the Uchiha clan," Zabuza said thoughtfully. *No wonder he's so strong...*

A cloud of mist began to form around

Zabuza. "So he may indeed be Haku's equal. No one has ever figured out Haku's moves until now. No one!"

Then Zabuza vanished into the fog once more.

9

"**HE'S GONE** again!" Sakura cried.

"Sakura, don't move an inch!" Kakashi warned. Zabuza could be anywhere in the mist.

"Okay," Sakura nodded.

"Do you hear me, Zabuza?" Kakashi called out. "Do you really think that I am only armed with the Sharingan? I too was a member of the Ninja Assassin Corps. I'll show you what kind of ninja I was once."

As Kakashi ran into the mist, Naruto

slowly raised his head. Sasuke had knocked him down, pushing him out of the way of Haku's attack. But what had happened to Sasuke?

He looked up to see Sasuke standing over him. His clothes were cut up by Haku's needles. Haku lay in a crumpled heap on the floor.

"No matter how many times I warn you, Naruto, you still keep getting in the way," Sasuke said, his voice hoarse.

Naruto smiled, relieved. "Sasuke, you're—"

Before he could finish, Sasuke collapsed. His face was as pale as the ice walls around them. Naruto was horrified.

"Get that lame expression off your stupid

face, you screwup," Sasuke said weakly.

He was trying to cover me, Naruto knew. "But why?"

Sasuke tried to think of an answer. Images of him and Naruto flashed through his head like scenes from a movie. Naruto bragging. Naruto showing off. Naruto screwing up...

"I used to hate you, you know," Sasuke said.

Naruto knew that already. "Then why did you...why me?"

Sasuke took a breath, and his lungs wheezed with the effort.

"How should I know?" Sasuke replied. "My body...just moved on its own!"

"You should have just minded your own business!" Naruto yelled.

Sasuke began to sway unsteadily. Naruto reached out and held him as he fell backward with a thud.

"I swore I wouldn't die…" Sasuke said, struggling for air. "…until I got revenge… revenge on my older brother. I thought that oath would save me. But it hasn't. Don't you dare die too, Naruto."

Sasuke's eyes closed. His face felt cold to the touch. Naruto's heart was pounding. Sasuke couldn't die now. He couldn't!

Something deep inside Naruto began to explode…

Haku slowly got to his feet. "He struck one blow at me and sacrificed himself for you," he told Naruto. "Such is a true ninja's path."

"Shut up," Naruto growled. He turned to

glare at Haku, and the ninja was shocked at the change in Naruto's face. His eyes were red, with pupils like black slits.

"I WILL STOP YOU!" he screamed. His voice shook with a sudden surge of power.

Angry orange flames rose up around Naruto. They circled him and Sasuke, rising higher and higher into the air. Then the flames began to take shape. The head of a snarling beast formed, a beast with glowing eyes and sharp, sharp teeth.

The Demon Fox sealed inside of Naruto was unleashed!

Ninja Terms

Hokage
The leader and protector of the Village Hidden in the Leaves. Only the strongest and wisest ninja can achieve this rank.

Jutsu
Jutsu means "arts" or "techniques." Sometimes referred to as *ninjutsu*, which means more specifically the jutsu of a ninja.

Bunshin
Translated as "doppelganger," this is the art of creating multiple versions of yourself.

Sensei
Teacher

Shuriken
A ninja weapon,
a throwing star

About the Authors

Author/artist **Masashi Kishimoto** was born in 1974 in rural Okayama Prefecture, Japan. After spending time in art college, he won the Hop Step Award for new manga artists with his manga *Karakuri* (Mechanism). Kishimoto decided to base his next story on traditional Japanese culture. His first version of *Naruto*, drawn in 1997, was a one-shot story about fox spirits; his final version, which debuted in *Weekly Shonen Jump* in 1999, quickly became the most popular ninja manga in Japan. This book is based on that manga.

......

Tracey West is the author of more than 150 books for children and young adults, including the *Pixie Tricks* and *Scream Shop* series. An avid fan of cartoons, comic books, and manga, she has appeared on the New York Times Best Seller List as the author of the Pokémon chapter book adaptations. She currently lives with her family in New York State's Hudson Valley.

The Story of Naruto continues in:
Chapter Book 7
The Next Level

Haku and Zabuza are the worst enemies Naruto and his friends have ever faced. Now that the battle has become a matter of life and death, Naruto must learn what it means to truly become a ninja: sometimes you have to fight to win… and then deal with the consequences.

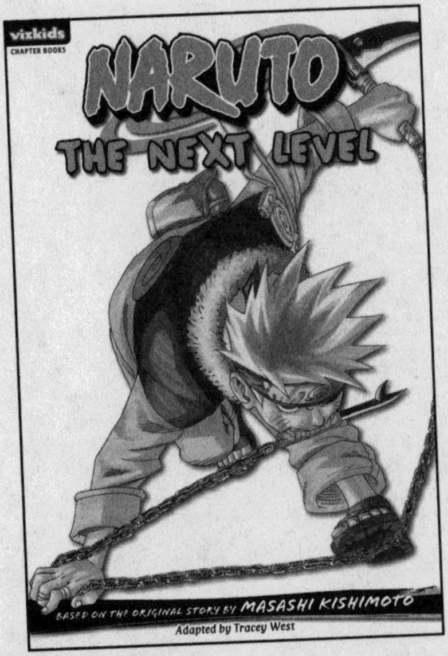
vizkids
CHAPTER BOOKS
NARUTO
THE NEXT LEVEL
BASED ON THE ORIGINAL STORY BY MASASHI KISHIMOTO
Adapted by Tracey West

COLLECT THEM ALL!
#1 THE BOY NINJA
#2 THE TESTS OF A NINJA
#3 THE WORST JOB
#4 THE SECRET PLAN
#5 BRIDGE OF COURAGE
#6 SPEED

COMING SOON!
#7 THE NEXT LEVEL

WANT TO HEAD BACK?

SURE!!

-:PUFF:-

-:PUFF:-